Terror of the Shivery Sea

Also by Ian Whybrow
and illustrated by Tony Ross

Little Wolf's Book of Badness
Little Wolf's Diary of Daring Deeds
Little Wolf, Forest Detective
Little Wolf's Haunted Hall for Small Horrors
Little Wolf, Pack Leader
Little Wolf's Postbag
Little Wolf's Handy Book of Peoms

First published by Collins in 2004
Collins is an imprint of HarperCollins*Publishers*
77-85 Fulham Palace Road, Hammersmith, London W6 8JB

The HarperCollins website address is www.harpercollins.co.uk
Little Wolf's website address is www.littlewolf.co.uk

1 3 5 7 9 8 6 4 2

0 00 715718 5

Printed and bound in Great Britain by
Clays Ltd, St Ives plc

IAN WHYBROW iLLUSTRATED BY TONY ROSS

LITTLE WOLF

Terror of the Shivery Sea

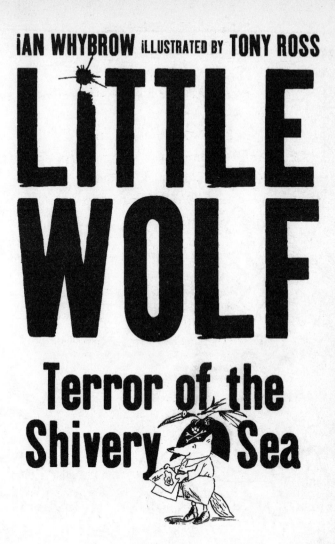

An imprint of HarperCollins*Publishers*

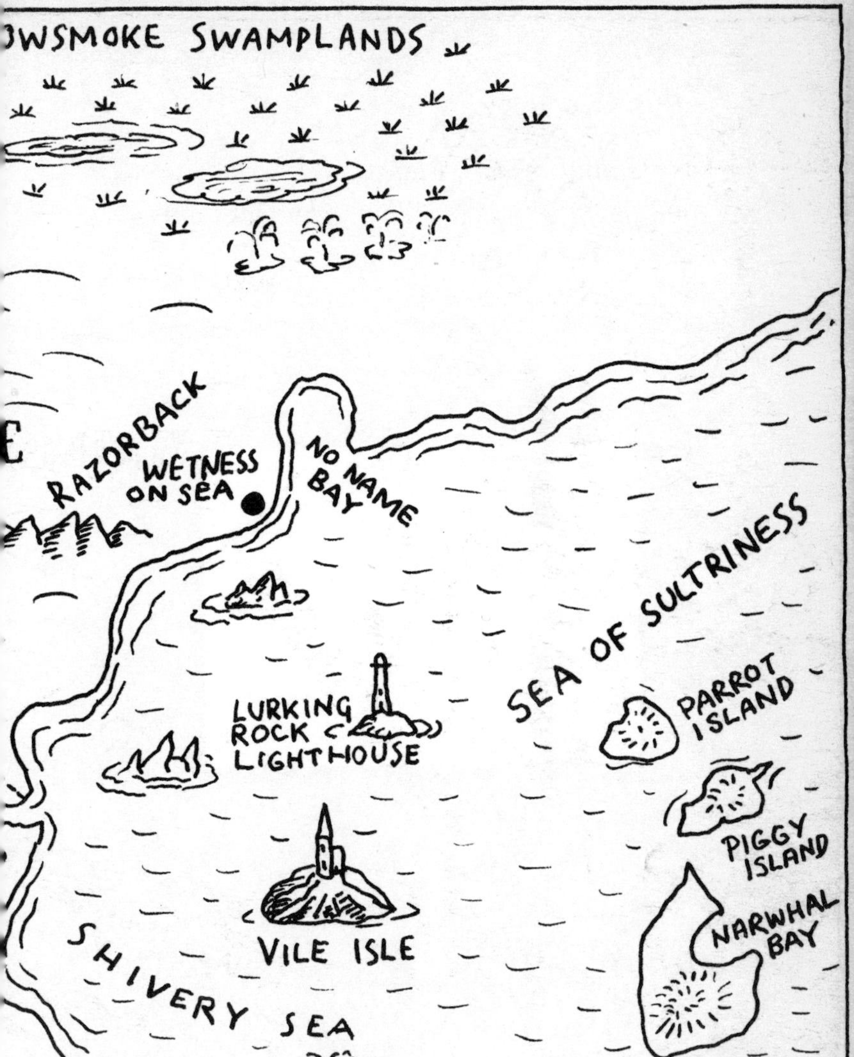

OWSMOKE SWAMPLANDS

RAZORBACK

WETNESS ON SEA

NO NAME BAY

SEA OF SULTRINESS

PARROT ISLAND

LURKING ROCK LIGHTHOUSE

PIGGY ISLAND

NARWHAL BAY

VILE ISLE

SHIVERY SEA

NARWHAL ISLAND

MILE

For my faithful readers, Marcus and Michael Powell
and for their grandad, Tom, who looks after
the lot of us.

Uncle Bigbad's **OLD PLACE**,
Frettnin Forest, Beastshire

My Desk

Dear Mum and Dad,

Please please PLEEEEEZ take Smells back to Murkshire to stay with you at the Lair. Go on, just for a short while, like ten years maybe, hint hint. You know he is your darling baby pet. Plus you are a lot fiercer than me, so you can stop him messing up your stuff.

Yeller wants me do Trick Practiss with him. Tricks is 1 of my best things, I love them, kiss kiss. BUT (big but) Smells keeps messing us about. Like if you are trying to have a private ~~conservash~~ ~~condensayshun~~ chat about fake bat poo or itchy powder, Smells keeps butting in hummingly.

Also, he pulls down his sailor suit bottoms saying, "Look at my pants, they got Stooffer the Steam Engine on them, nar nar!" Just because he is jealous of my pants saying Wiggly World, I bet.

So cubbish.

I wish wish **wishhhh** you would take him back, because now he has got a habit of going **B l a h   B l a h** in a loud way till you play Doctor Monster with him. He makes you be ill in bed so he can do harsh operations on you that really hurt.

You have him for a bit, go on, he is your cub. I am only his big bruv, so not fair, eh?

Yours snugglupply,

L Wolf, Son Numero Un (french)

Uncle Bigbad's **OLD PLACE**, Frettnin Forest, Beastshire

Kitchen Table

Dear Mum and Dad,

You have not replied to my letter about taking Smells back. I know you have been having a nice long winter hibernate, so maybe it is best to say my chums' names for you in a xplainy way. (Just in case of your branes being shut down still, OK?)

Now (xplainy voice) my best friend and cuz is Yeller Wolf, hmmm? He has got loads of BIG IDEAS and shouts a lot.

My next best friends are Normus Bear
(wopping mussels)

plus Stubbs Crow (clever beak,
says "ARK!" a lot).

These are some
adventures we have
done before, OK?

turn over

🐾 Daring Deeds at Adventure Academy.

🐾 Haunting at Haunted Hall with dead Uncle Bigbad as our Top Ghost. (He died of eating 2 many bakebeans 2 fast and went off bang, remember?)

🐾 Being Frettnin Forest Detective Agency, that was good.

🐾 Camping out, tracking ect. with me being Pack Leader.

Now we are trying to think up another fine adventure to have, but Smells is spoiling it for us, NOT FAIR.

Yours remindingly,

L Wolf, Son

Uncle Bigbad's **OLD PLACE**,
Frettnin Forest, Beastshire

Down The Coalhole

Dear Mud and Dam,

Thank you for your sharp note saying pack up reminding people. Also you do not like me saying about your brane being shut down, so I must lock myself in the coalhole for cheek. OK, but serve you right if this writing is on the wonk (dark in here).

About saying "Yes?" and "Hmmm?" and all that. You say that is a big sauce, talking to you in a xplainy way. Because you are big parents, not small weaky fluffballs, so now I must suck a bar of soap, OR ELSE. Plus I must *pack in whining* and saying *not fair*.

OK, I will count myself lucky being able to spend time with my baby bruv, but can you check your clock to see how long that time is? I think it has got stuck.

Yours punishedly,

Little Filth (coaldust)

PS I have not done the soapsucking part yet. Sorry, but I cannot do my best writing plus spitting out bubbles at the same time.

PPS I am doing it now, spit spit, bluck.

Uncle Bigbad's **OLD PLACE,**
Frettnin Forest, Beastshire

Drawer Number 3 (ahh cosy),
Chester Draws, My Room

Dear Mum and Dad,

Shame about Dad catching a touch of the Mange, so now he is all germy. You say Smellybreff cannot come near Dad for ages, in case he might catch it. His fur will go itchy and drop off in rugsize lumps, oo-er.

Yes, I understand Dad is being noble in a wolfly way. (If he is not telling a wopping FAT FIB, hint hint.)  By the way, is the Mange like blancMange? Because you never get fur on that either, funny, eh? Only if you leave it out of the fridge for a week.

Yours askingly,

Son wun

Dear M and D,

You know when I was down the coalyhole sucking soap for getting on your nerves? Well I found a dusty old pic chucked out by Uncle Bigbad, a big 1 with a posh frame.

I thought, I know, give it a bit of a soapy lick, see who is under the dust. Then I found out. It is a fearsum old wolf plus beard, scar ect., all covered in guns and daggers! He has got a funny hat on with a mutton bones badge made out of jewels, all sparkly like his earring. He has got a crool, teasy look on his face, plus he is sitting on a big strong old chest. In his paw he is holding a long twisty stick, looks like coff candy, only made of elephant tusks, maybe.

I gave the notice underneath a good shine up on my fur so you can see some words, they are:

Blackfur the Backbiter.

I wonder who that Blackfur was. I bet he was an olden day park-keeper that was all snarl and snappish, yes?

Yours surmisingly,

Detective Inspectickles Wolf
(get it?)

PS Clue: no it is me
wearing spectickles
really.

Sofa, Sitting Room.

Dear Mum and Dad,

Surmisingly is not a trick word, it is a real 1, honest. I found it in a detecting book. So I thought, go on, give it a short tryout in your next letter.

Sorry it made Dad go Grrrr, but maybe that was just his normal temper. Or the Mange, maybe. Or sitting on a hedgehog.

19

Thank you for your answer to the pic I found down the coalyhole. I have hung it in the Hall now because you say it is a Family Portrait of our grate wolfly ancestor Blackfur the Rat Pie, Terror of All the Sea.

No wonder Uncle Bigbad got jealous and chucked him away. Uncle did not want anywun to know there was a bigger Terror than him, I bet!

1 small thing I still do not get is how can a Rat Pie be a Terror of anything? I love rat pies (yum yum, not scary 1 bit).

Yours puzzledly,

Little

Tree Stump, Up The Garden.

Dear Mum and Dad,

Still no news from you about rat pies, boo shame.

I am writing this in pencil, but do not sing:

Nar Nar bubbacub, You are just a blubbercub.

You know I hate doing writing in pencil, but it is all Smells' fault. Today is my worst day this week, because of Smells meeting a raccoon with a mask on in Frettnin Forest. After that he got jealous, saying he wanted to have a mask 2 and be Mister Burgle-Arrr the Robber.

I 'spect you will say, "Oh well done, Smellybreff, my fine baby cub, now you are following in Daddy's pawprints." But listen, Yeller and me said well done to him 2! We said, "Fine, well done, you *can* be a burgle-arrr, Smells. But only if you stick to robbing ants, piggies ect. OK?"

Sad to say, he did not listen. He went and robbed all my furniture and hid it. So now no bed to sleep on, no chester draws ect. Plus Smells drinking all my ink just for spitefulness. Floors are my worst thing for sleeping on, so it made me get up stiffly in the morningtime needing a warmupp trot outside. Off I went joggingly, then guess what? A **BIG** moose came rushing! He tried to kill me dead with his horns, a **BIG** moose! All because of Smells robbing his grass off him!

Yours moaningly,

Little

PS Good thing Normus came along and gave that moose a hard bash.

Uncle Bigbad's **OLD PLACE,**
Frettnin Forest, Beastshire

My Bed again, hmmm snuggly,
My Room

Dear Mum and Dad,

Today I feel a lot
more cheery because of
finding a big haystack
by Beech Grove. Only
it was not a haystack
really, it was my
furniture buried
in moose grass
by Smells.

Also, a big *Arrrroooo!* to Smells for stopping
messing me about (mostly). That is because he
has gone all soppy over Normus for having big
mussels and bashing that moose. (By the way, it
was kwite tasty, lipsmack, lipsmack.)

23

Now Smells is busy outside playing Jack and the Cabbagestalk with Normus. Smells lets both of them be the Giant-bashers, so Normus likes it 2. Sometimes they creep up behind people, going bonk.

I was that people 1 time so I said a loud *Ouch!* Then Smells went and cuddled Normus's leg, saying to me, "Be quiet, I hate you Little. I only like Normus now!"

Funny, I did not know he liked me before. Oh well, never mind, as long as he leaves me alone. Now I can have a quiet readupp and maybe find a nice new adventure to have.

By the way, I got your short card saying **WAKE UP!!!!** Plus saying, "Your faymuss ancestor Blackfur was a Pie Rat not a Rat Pie, you Blunking Blip ect. Plus he was sitting on a chest full of treasure, so get out of bed and go and find it NOW!"

Sorry, I still do not get it. What does that mean, Pie Rat?

Yours headscratchingly,

Little Dimp

Dear Mum and Dad,

Oh, I get it now. Blackfur was a Pie Rat spelt PIRATE! I asked Stubbs and he said, "ARK!" meaning look it up in the en*zark*lopedia. So we did. Sad to say, I only read a short part because just then, Smells came by being Jack and the Cabbagestalk. So he chopped up the page I was reading with his chopper, then he ate it saying:

"Bee By Bo Bum,
I like paper, yum yum yum."

Not funny.

Normus said, "Hoy, be fair Smells – no bashing pages. Save bashing for big giants." Smells did not like Normus telling him off, so he chopped up his trout net saying, "Be quiet, I hate you, Normus. I only like Yeller now!"

I said (wise voice), "There, I told you he was only a short friend, Normus."
That is Y Normus has gone off for a sulk.
I can hear him outside hitting trees - *bonk*, e e - a r r r, **crash**.

Lucky Yeller still wants to be my chum.

Yours tuttingly,

Little Cheesedoff

Dear Mum and Dad,

Soon I will have no friends left. It is all your fault because of making me look after your crool baby. Also, how can I find Blackfur's treasure when I have to keep doing cub-sitting for my baby bruv?

Did I say about Smells wanting to be Mister Tricker, yes? Also about him having a big crush on Yeller for showing him loads of good tricks, yes? Trouble is, Smells only likes trying them out on me eg.:

The Fridge Trick

Smells comes running
into the kitchen saying,
"Hello, Little, is your
fridge running? Good,
now it is running out
the window." Then he
chucks it out saying,
"Har har tricked you!"

Another eg.

This morning, Smells swallowed a big load of my Lego bits. Then he pressed his tummy button and sicked them all up saying, "Look, me a toaster, pop, pop!"

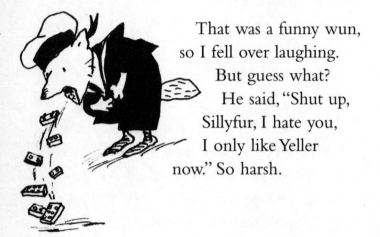

That was a funny wun, so I fell over laughing. But guess what? He said, "Shut up, Sillyfur, I hate you, I only like Yeller now." So harsh.

Yours jealously,

Little

PS I am 2 upsett to xplain now, so more tomorrow.

Dear Mum and Dad,

Here are Yeller's last words that he said to me doorslammingly, (in a note, he rolled them up then skwashed them up my keyhole).

LISTEN LICKLE, I AM ALL FED UP. I TRIED BEIN NICE TO SMELLS, HIM BEIN ONLY A TITCH, BUT NOW HE AS GORN 2 FAR. HE KEPT ON PESTERIN ME TO TEACH HIM MORE AND MORE TRICKS. SO IN THE END, I THOUGHT, I KNOW, I WILL TRY TO DOUBLE-TRICK HIM. SO I SAID, "SMELLS, YOU ARE SUCH A GOOD TRICKER, SO YOU MUST NEVER, NEVER, NEVER PLAY MISTER TIDYUPP, OK?" THAT MADE HIM GO ALL CRAFTY-LOOKIN.

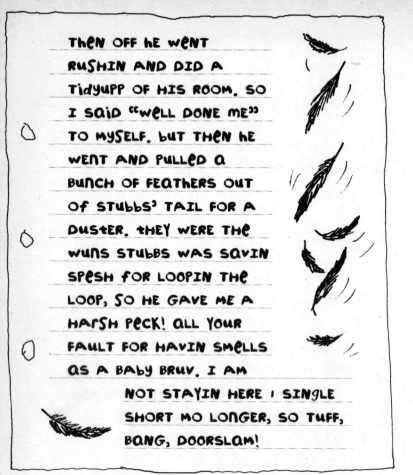

THEN OFF HE WENT
RUSHIN AND DID A
TIDYUPP OF HIS ROOM. SO
I SAID "WELL DONE ME"
TO MYSELF. BUT THEN HE
WENT AND PULLED A
BUNCH OF FEATHERS OUT
OF STUBBS' TAIL FOR A
DUSTER. THEY WERE THE
WUNS STUBBS WAS SAVIN
SPESH FOR LOOPIN THE
LOOP, SO HE GAVE ME A
HARSH PECK! ALL YOUR
FAULT FOR HAVIN SMELLS
AS A BABY BRUV. I AM
NOT STAYIN HERE 1 SINGLE
SHORT MO LONGER, SO TUFF,
BANG, DOORSLAM!

And now Stubbs just hid up the chimney
saying, "ARK!" meaning he will never darken
my doorknob again.

Yours leftalonely,

L ect. (2 upsett to write all of my
name down proply, so there)

Dear Mum and Dad,

I am all sad without Yeller and Normus here, but good news about Stubbs. He did not like me going snifful parp ect. in my hanky, so out of the chimney hole he popped with a nice present (beakful of crawlycreeps for a snack). Then off he went  flappingly down the shop and fetched me a copy of *Wolf Weekly*, so he and me could have a nice newsy read together.

Guess what we read in the paper? There is ANOTHER Terror of the Seas. They say he is even more of a Terror than our ancestor Blackfur the Backbiter. This 1 is called Captain Froshus. Oo-er!

Stubbs has cut this story out for you with his clever beak. Do you like it? It has got some fine ~~dizgiz deskies~~ (cannot spell it) dressing up in it.

Your own cub reporter (get it?)

Little Wolf

Terror on the Shivery Sea

Once again, the mysterious Captain Froshus, Master of *The Seafox* is gaining a reputation as the most ruthless and terrifying pirate ever to sail The Shivery Sea.

cunning disguise

It is said that Captain Froshus has gathered a harsh crew that includes polecats, stoats and vicious wild boars to do his dirty work. They specialize in cunning disguise, so for the moment, the true identity of the captain and crew remain cloaked in secrecy.

witness speaks

Meanwhile, yesterday, three miles off No-name Bay, *The Seafox* captured two fishing-boats: *The Kipper* and *The Slippery Eel*. Ricky Walruss, mate of *The Kipper*, spoke to our reporter, once he was safely aboard the Swamplands lifeboat.

"We had no chance!" he said. "We was just having a bit of a trawl, like, when we seen this schooner sailing up astern. She must have been lurking up a creek somewhere. We didn't take much notice, seeing her crew was no more than a parcel of girlies wearing flowery dresses. Then snip my flipper if she didn't hoist the Snarl and Wishbones and shoot our rudder off with a cannon ball! Then she come right alongside and after that it was Swish

Swush Sploosh till I wound up in the drink, minus me wallet and me watch!"

victim tells all

Just before going to press, *Wolf Weekly* has learned from one of the victims of *The Slippery Eel*, Able Sealion 'Honks' Greymuzzle, that for several hours, he was questioned at pistol-point by Captain Froshus himself. The Captain kept asking what the Able Sealion knew about the hidden treasure of the legendary pirate, Blackfur the Backbiter. Recovering last night in a warm cabin in Riggly Creek, the stunned victim told our reporter that he knew nothing about any hidden treasure or any pirate called Blackfur the Backbiter. Asked to describe Captain Froshus,

Able Sealion Greymuzzle said that he couldn't see his face because he was wearing a mask. However, *he spoke very softly, had big staring eyes and smelt strongly of pepper.*

warning!

Be warned, readers! No vessel, brute beast or seaside home is safe from the heartless ways of these wicked plunderers. And the shaming fact is that among the whole shocking crew there is not one single wolf!

Editorial: p 15:
Running Out of Huff? Modern Wolves Slip Down the Most Wicked List

Low Branch, Oak Tree, Near Home

Dear Em and Dee,

Thank you for your
very fast package saying:

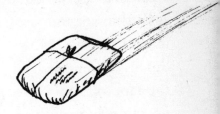

"Hurry up and set Smells a good example
Pack up doing cissie reading and Run Away To
Sea THIS MINUTE!!!"

You say I MUST FIND that lost treasure of
Blackfur's for you sharply before that Captain
Froshus gets his paws on it. But, if Captain Froshus
finds it 1ˢᵗ, it is up to me to get it off him, so that I
keep up our fearsum family name of Wolf.

Yes, I got the tape of you singing. You say it is
an old pack song, sposed to be from Blackfur's
time. It goes:

> **Seek my treasure in the bay,**
> **Where the unicorn doth play!**
> **Those who seek without a map,**
> **Mind the teeth that snarl and snap!**
> **Lucky those who most do itch,**
> **Scratch, and lo, ye shall be rich!**

37

Har har, good joke because listen to the funny
words. Also, even bubbercubs know there is no
such thing as unicorns, they are just a ~~lejunds~~
ledgend stories. Now
Smells has burgled
the tape off me so
he can play it on his
Walkwolf and do
dancing.

Yes, I do understand the most *important* part of
your message. The bit about how all that gold
and jewels ect. belong to you really because you
are the nearest ancestors to Blackfur in the Wolf
family, yes? That xplains the foamy photo of
himself that Dad sent. I thought, funny, I did not
know Dad liked shaving. But no, he was not
shaving, he was just frothing keenly at the mouth
being greedy, sorry.

You say, addingly, a Mind You like this: "Mind You, it is a bit 2 dangerous for our darling baby pet Smellybreff to go Running Away To Sea, in case he might get killed or worse." I must seek my sulky chums swiftly and pass on this message from you. It is: "Hoy, Yeller, Normus and Stubbs, pack in being hopeless and make yourself a bit useful. Grrrrr, you stay put, then you can be guards for our Smellybreff."

OK, I will try my hardest to make up with them, but I think Yeller and Normus have gone right off me (all because of Youknowwho).

Yours seekingly

The Panter

Dear Mum and Dad,

It is hard work keeping up
our fearsum name of Wolf,
so now I am having a
sitdown on a short heap
of pine needles. My
chums must be having
a curlupp down a
deep hole or a cave
somewhere. I have
looked and looked and
still no luck.

Will you send me EVERYTHING you know
about Blackfur and Pirate Ways? Smells ate my
pirate page out of the encyclopedia, remember,
and no good me chasing after Blackfur's treasure
cluelessly, eh? Maybe you have got a treasure
map tucked up a drawer somewhere, hmmm?

Your hunting son,

Little Beagle

Indoors again, by stained glass window
with magnifying glass, Big Hall

Dear Mum

No map from you, boo shame, never mind. But Mum, can you do the writing next time? Dad's ~~skwigs skrorl~~ scribble joined-up letters are a bit 2 rushing for me. (Just because he cannot wait to have a gloat over *that lost* treasure, I bet.)

I have had a good go at reading Dad's tips about Blackfur and Pirate Ways, but it is hard for small eyes. I think I get the 1st bit. It says Dad does not know much about Blackfur, so shut up asking. Then the next bit goes something like: "They add windy botts." Does Dad mean pirates used the strong wind to sail their *boats*? I hope so, if not, hold your noses, phew.

Also:
- What is, "Ho yoyo and a bobble of rug?"
- How does he mean "welking the plonk?"
- Dad says (I think), "Pirates like capturing loads of booties." Why? Have they got heaps of babies with chilly feet?
- Is he sure about, "Snotted hankies round their heads?" (Errrr, rude habits!)
- Dad, do you mean pirates *do* big pants or they *wear* big pants?
- Also how can you chop people's heads off with 'cute lass'?

Yours onlyaskingly,

Little

Uncle Bigbad's OLD PLACE,
Frettnin Forest, Beastshire

Boot Room, just next to The Pantry

Dear Dad,

Sorry, I forgot, Dad wolves are not sposed to write proply. Also they do not like keeping on saying answers. So tuff luck me, I must find out about Blackfur plus pirate ways bymyselfly. Plus, I must get out on the seawater and find Blackfur's treasure AT WUNCE before the shocking foe (eg. Captain Froshus) gets it.

Oh yes, also I must wind up the clockwork botty-booter you sent and bend over. Good idea, I think Yeller and Normus might come back for a demonstrayshun of that. Yeller likes trick machines and Normus likes doing pain on people.

Yours ouchly

Ivor Bootedbott
(get it?)

Dear Mum and Dad,

Arrroooo! This morning, Yeller and Normus
came out of their hidyhole rushingly to watch
the botty-booter go doof-doof. Yeller thinks it is
kwite good, a bit like the chin-tickler he made
out of a lectric fan 1 time. Only his machine was
a bit more har-hary than ouch-ouchy. Yeller
wanted to take the botty-booter apart with his
screwdriver, only Normus said it was rubbish
and booted it back (jealous) so now it is up near
Windy Ridge, I bet.

They both say Not Fair they cannot Run
Away to Sea with me to find the treasure. But I
think they know deepdownly that they must stay
here. Hope so, because who else will protect
Smells xcept them when I go?

Guess what? Yeller had a Big Idea just now! He said we must do Pirate Rules, plus ship training on Lake Lemming for the practiss of sea habits. Arrroooo! All because he had read LOADS about pirates. He did not say so before because of being in a mood.

Yours studyingly,

Uncle Bigbad's **OLD PLACE**,
Frettnin Forest, Beastshire

Concrete bit for parking sheds on, Garden

Dear Mum and Dad,

I have done you a nice pic of us dressed up as
pirates on our small ship we just made. The
ship is a bit rubbish because of being made
out of an old shed plus garden tools, but good
costumes, hmmm?

Can you see the pirate with the eye patch? Hem hem, that is me! Yeller, Normus and Stubbs have just got hankies on, (but they are *spotty* not *snotty*, Dad, OK)? Smells hates hankies, he only wants to wear his normal sailor suit plus droopy moustache plus his airgun. That is Y the sail is a bit holey.

You know that piece of paper all funny round the edges? (Hint, came in the envelope with this.) Stubbs made that for you spesh. It is our Pirate Rules in proper old-fashy writing, done with a feather going dippy-dip in the ink, nice and splutty.

RULES FOR ~~Pie-Rats~~ PIRATES

※ Pirates must do SST (Surprise, Speed and Terror) so people will go, "Oo-er, what is that? Oh no, help, 2 late, captured."

※ Only 1 Cheef Captain (L Wolf) doing the orders (boss about).

※ Pirate packs are called crews. The important ones get posh names, eg. Bosun (Yeller), Steerybear and Lasher (Normus), Lookout (Stubbs), Gunner (Smells) ect.

※ Crew must say, "Eye-eye Captain" a lot, plus singing, "Ho yoyo and a bobble of rug", like Dad said.

※ BUT (big but) crews get to vote about harsh orders, plus sharing grub, booties, treasure ect. (Yeller's idea).

※ If you are a deserter or scaredycub, you get macarooned on a boring island with nobody to eat.

※ No mutiny or you get lashes off Normus Bear plus a long walk off a short floorboard.

Good, eh?

Yours fullspeedaheadly,

The Pirate Cheef

Dear Mum and Dad,

Today we did a lawnch of the good ship *Sheddy* and off we went for a fine sail by Coot Island. It is up the reedy end of Lake Lemming, in case you did not know.

It took *Sheddy* a long time because of going in circles, banging into things ect. Shame about bears being heavy. Because if you are the Steerybear you have to sit by the rudder at the back end, meaning Normus tips up me and my crew in the air, so a bit hard for him sailing straight (cannot see).

Also, he gets grumpy about us saying, "Mind out, Normus, go this way, no go that way," all the time. It says in Yeller's book what Steerybears are sposed to do if they want to do Going About (eg. turn round the other way).

Number 1 is, point where you want to go plus shouting out, "Stand by to Go About!" Number 2 is, just before the sail comes flying over the other side, shout out "Lee Ho" (chineez meaning "Duck").

Only our sail keeps being 2 quick, it comes over whizzingly and hits him 1. So Normus goes, "Hoy! Pack that in!" and hits it back. Now it is even more holey than from Smells shooting it, boo shame.

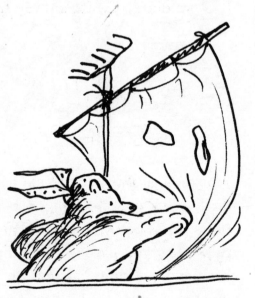

Sad to say, we did a big crash into Coot Island.

But 1 good thing, we did SST (Surprise Speed and Terror) after all, because then many a coot hopped off flappingly doing loud cooty noises! Plus we did that without even trying. Good eh?

Arrrrooooo!

Yours hoyoyoly,

Little Wolf, P.C.

(Clue: not Pleece Constabull, not Personal Computer, not Piece of Cheese. Go on, have a guess.)

Dear Mum and Dad,

More pirate practiss this morning, just after sunjumpup, but no luck capturing pirate victims. There is not much of them round Lake Lemming, only ducks, but they're a bit 2 quick for us. Boo shame, I love roast duck, kiss kiss. Wunce we did creeping up on a pelican, saying (piratey voice), "Heave 2, matey, and let's be having your beakful of fish or we sink you, a-harrr!" But not

fair, he just gave me a sharp peck on the nose. Plus swallowing Yeller's trick sword that he made spesh.

We had a fine short lunch. It says in Yeller's book about how pirates like eating hard tacks with weevils in. We did not eat many tacks

(2 sharp) but not to wurry because there are plenty of weevils tucked up in the cracks of the *Sheddy* (nice and juicy, yum yum!). That got our strongness up for being Terrors, so hup with our anchor and hup with our sail and off we went rockingly.

Kwite soonly, we came to the north shore. Stubbs was up the front being the Lookout so he said, "ARK!" times 3, meaning "H*ark*, maties! Otters l*ark*ing about off the st*ark*board bow!"

Yeller yelled, "AHOY YOU LUBBERS. GIVE US A GO ON YOUR MUDSLIDE A-HARRR, OR YOU SHARL BE GETTIN A TASTE OF CHILLY STEEL UP YOUR VITALS!" But they just swam under water and bot our ship's bittom (other way round, sorry).

Yours sunkly,

Little Glugglug.

Dear Bubb add Dadd,

I hab got a small cold id by doze, shame eh? It is all those otters' fault for making us get sunk. Normus likes going in the water because of his hobby (trout tickling) but it makes me and Yeller go ~~hallerjick~~ ~~oo-ergie~~ all

funny. Still, we are not giving up, so Arrroooo! times 3 for our braveness. Plus Arrrroooo to Stubbs for cooking us some nice warm Micemince Tarts 2 eat (only he calls them t*ark*s).

Here is some more cheery news. Normus found a punt in the bullrushes. Do you know punts? They have got a flat bott and you push them by a pole (no sails) so handier for pirately SST practiss on ducks.

54

Only 1 prob. Smells has been down the cellar and guess what? He found a short fat old musket of Uncle Bigbad's, plus rusty old flintlock pistol plus gunpowder. He hates airguns now, he only wants to do blunderbusses.

We said he could tie the blunderbuss on the front of the punt (or is it frunt of the pont?) but not 2 much bangs, OK?

More later.

Yours ah-choooly,

Diddle Boolf

PS Sorry about the sneezy bits (chewed micemince).

Dear Mum and Dad,

I am having to write this quietly (tickly throat plus ache in my head).

We did pirate practiss in the punt yesterday but it was rubbish because of Smells putting a whole cupful of gunpowder up his musket in 1 go. Not funny, because we were just punting along nice and creepingly up to some tasty ducks riding on the water.

Normus did not sit on the back end this time, he had a lie-down instead. Then he held up a mirror so he could see the way to steer, plus doing the rudder part with his back feet. Yeller and Stubbs had to skwash down on top of him, no wiggling. I did the poling, Smells did being the Gunner up the front.

I wanted to shout, "Heave 2 you ducks, pirates here, so surrender up 4 nice eggs no messing!" but my voice went wrong. It was so weaky with my cold, it would not come out of its hole proply. So quick as a chick, Smells did a command saying: "Wings up, ducks. BANG!" like that with his blunderbuss, only louder.

That bang made our punt rush back rocketly across the lake! Then bonk into a willow tree and splash into the wetness wunce morely.

Yours streamingly

The patient

PS Smells never misses.

PPS Now I have got a coff, thanks Smells very much I do not think.

PPPS I am sending you a tape of my coff going kuh kuh kuh kuh, case you do not believe me.

Road to the Sea, Banks of River Riggly,
Gravelly Bit, West of Hazardous Canyon

Dear Mum and Dad,

Today me and Stubbs did *proper* Running Away To Sea! Normus and Yeller have helped me pack my kitbag with snacks, ect. I am ~~in disgizz,~~ ~~disgize~~ (still cannot spell it) wearing my pretend pirate costume of eyepatch, peggy leggy ect. Also Stubbs has got red and yellow paint on (eg. like a parrot). He can say "ARK!" meaning Pieces of *Ark*, get it? He is a good parrot.

Smells is tucked up sulkingly in his cot, covered in spots. It might be the chickypops from eating 2 many chickies.

Yeller and Normus say, yes, they will look after him. BUT (big but), I think they are grumpy underneath because of me not letting them come on our xciting Search. They hate me again, I bet.

No more coffs, no more reading, no more pirate practiss, just danger for me and Stubbs. Hope you are happy now. Also, this is my last letter probly. So a dew! (French)

Yours runawaytosealy,

Able Seawolf Little

Dear Parents of Little Wolf,

Bad **N**ews. I am not killed yet.
(Wait, that is not the bad news, sorry. I just put the Bad News part down 1st. It took me a long time doing the big B and the N, so I forgot my real news I wanted to say, OK?) Do not fret and frown, the real Bad News is coming up next, here it is for you, ready, go.

Bad News (real). Smells has ~~dissobay~~ ~~disobb~~ not done what you said he must do. You know he went to bed with the chickypops? Well that was not him, that was his ted. Smells just tucked his ted up in his cot and plopped red dots on him. He got the red dots off my best clicky biro that he knows he is not sposed to touch, in case he might wear it out! I think he robbed that off me when he had that craze about being a burgle-arrr, remember?

That is how I found out about him being a stowaway in my kitbag. Something kept going clicky-click all the time, in between my peggy leggy going kerlonk kerlonk down the road. It was Smells!

So anyway, it is nice having my clicky biro back, even if I do have to take Smells with me now to seek Blackfur's treasure, ect. Because if I do not, you will only say moaningly that I am a slow sluggy slowcoach for not Running Away To Sea my fastest.

Yours zoomingly,

Little Russia (like rusher, get it?)

PS Stubbs says "ARK!" meaning he is arkay

Dear Mum and Dad,

Sorry about no letters for 3 days. We just kept
on rushingly, right through Hazardous Canyon
(2 much rushy water, bbbrrr), then under
Funder Falls (wet paws all the time, plus soggy
peggy leggy, boo shame). Next we went across
the south bit of the White Wildness. Wun time
we got snowwhite all over but it was not funny.
Also we got sore bits from frostnip that the wind
did (by throwing sharp sleet at us crossing
the Razorback).

Then up jumped the sun when we got near the coast. It was not turned up to its hottest but it made us a lot more cheery. We followed the coast path northly till we nearly got to the end of Grimshire. Then we came to a cliffy part, that is the south side of Noname Bay, just by Wetness-on-Sea. Next we had a lie-down in the warm grass, hmmmm nice.

Then, after a lovely pant, plus watching some ships going past on the sea, down we marched watchingly into the little town, saying a marching poem:

"Blackfur's Treasure, we are after you.
Captain Froshus watch out 2.
Grrr, grrr, grrr,
Plus a loud Arrrrrooooo!"

Do you like our trick pic? It is not fat ladies. It is me, Smells and Stubbs really.

Wetness is nice for wolves, plus Stubbs likes all the gulls going "EEEEK", he says they are *ark*ceptional. My peggy leggy got 2 hot, so off I popped it into my kitbag for now. But my eyepatch is still on, just in case.

Smells likes the sea. It is all blue and wet, a bit like Lake Lemming, only somebody put a load of salt in it, spit spit! The sand is nice 2, only it is good for burying people, worse luck, because guess what Smells' new hobby is? Digging!

Yours uptomyneckly,

L

PS No pirates round here.

Dear Mum and Dad,

Me and Stubbs wanted to get tracking today. Stubbs kept saying cawingly "ARK!" times 4, meaning let us get b*ark* on the tr*ark* of the treasure of Bl*ark*fur and take it b*ark* where it belongs. But Smells made us go to Whizzland, by going screamy scream scream if we did not spoil him rotten.

We dug a hole under the fence to get in (no money) and guess where we came up? The

Ghostie Train tunnel. It was funny. Plus we won the game because we were the scaryest.

When we popped up, all the other people went, "Help, mummy, oo-er!" Then off they ran screamingly, har har!

The roller-coaster was funny 2 if
you love being sick like Smells does.
But my best was the Flea Circus. It
had flea ballet-dancers with feathers
on, fleas pulling chariots,
plus fleas riding their bikes
ect. I said to the man, "Do you
have Flea Restling?" He said
replyingly, "No." So me and
Smells went scratchy-
scratch in our fur and I said,
"You have now!" Out jumped a
small pack of our
own fleas, and
into the ring they ran
hoppingly to give those circus
fleas a good fight!

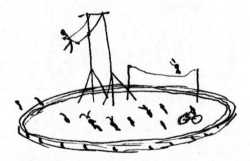

We thought that was the best part, but the man was crool, saying, "Hoy, buzz off you itchy blunkers and take that scrawny parrot with you ect!"

Stubbs said, "ARK!" meaning do not be sarky about parrots. That was a good insult for a short crow, yes? Then guess what? We won a goldfish yum yum, tasty. It was on the Test Your Strongness with a Big Hammer game. We were a bit 2 weaky at 1st because we could not make the dinger go up and hit the bell. But then Stubbs sat on it. So next time we went dong on the button with the hammer, Stubbs did just 1 small flippy-flap and up he went and hit the bell with a loud donk!

DONK

But that winning-a-goldfish trick was not Y
we got chucked out of Whizzland, oh no! That
was because of Smells winning all the dollies at
the shooting gallery going bullseye, bullseye,
bullseye. He never misses.

So now we are off down the harbour to have
a proper look for Blackfur clues. No ~~sine sing~~
sign of unicorns in bays yet. Or people having an
itch. Maybe that song was a just pretend 1?
Remember?

Seek my treasure in the bay,
Where the unicorn doth play!

We are being v. careful and hiding from
anywun who looks like Captain Froshus and
smells of pepper.

Yours dollydupply,

LW

Below Deck, The Saucy Sardine,
Somewhere on The Shivery Sea

Dear Mum and Dad,

You know we went down the harbour? Well that is a posh name for a place where they keep fishing boats on leads. So I thought, hmmm, good place for Running Away To Sea. Also, to find out what tricks that Captain Froshus has been up to. So we can think of a better way to **SCARE** him, if he finds the treasure before us.

Soon we saw a boat painted green (my best colour). Plus it had a fine name, **The Saucy Sardine.** Also, it had a big notice saying:

So up the gangplank we went saying, "Ah-harrr," ect. to the small cheery man doing mending on his fishing net. He said to us, "Ahoy there, mateys. And what be you a-doing aboard *The Saucy Sardine*? I be the skipper by the way."

So I said (sailory voice), "Good joke, matey, because where be your skipping rope?" But then he said, "Oh no, I be the *captain*." So *I* said, "Me and my chums here, we be looking for work."

The captain said, "Ho yes? That do make a nice change. Most deckhands are too frit to sign on for a voyage, because of that Captain Froshus and his wicked crew."

I said, "We be not frit, matey, we be tuff. And, we be not deckhands, ah-harrr. But if you be looking for deck*paws,* then we have got strong wuns, plus my parrot chum here has got a strong deck*beak.* Also, I have got my own peggy leggy in this kitbag!"

So the captain said, "Well nibble me ratlines – I like the cut of your jibs! I be Captain Bold, so welcome aboard. Now jump to it lively and stow your dunnage! We sail on the afternoon tide."

Yours crewly,

A Fisher (get it?)

PS I found out 'dunnage' is a sailor word for 'stuff', good eh?

Dear Mum and Dad,

It is good being a deckpaw if you do not mind scrubbing decks or getting many a skwirt from Smells doing the hosing. Captain Bold is a fine teacher. Plus he likes having us around saying, "Eye-eye Captain," then helping with stowing, steering, heave-hoes, hupp-she-rises, swabbing ect.

Me and Smells are good at cleaning out fish barrels. This is how we do it. Jump in a barrel, do a hedgehog-curlupp, then a spinny-spin. We are so quick, you would not bel*eeeeev*! Also Stubbs is brilliant at mending nets with his clever beak. He keeps saying "ARK! ARK!" meaning netw*arking* is *ark*cellent fun.

Catching sardines from boats is good. You catch them by a trick that is so *easy cheesy*! 1ˢᵗ you just throw a big net over the back on a long strong string. Then all the fishes go, "Hmm, swimming in all this sea is 2 boring, come on, let us have a ~~challunj~~ go at wiggling through those teeny weeny holes. Oh no, help, my fins are stuck, boo shame." So now double helpings of grub for us, Arrroooo!

You know that far part on the end of the sea where the sky comes down? That is called the horizon. It has got a hansum sailing ship on it.

Yours spottingly,

Sharpeye

Dear Mum and Dad,

Oo-er, you know that hansum sailing ship? Up it sailed swiftly, quiet as a cat. Captain Bold said mutteringly, "What be that lubber's game? If she don't watch herself, she'll find herself all a-hoo and tangled in our net! Quick boys, get out the Signals Book and check them fancy flags she's a-flying."

So quick as a chick I checked, saying, "Eye-eye, Skipper, that signal means Have a Nice Day!"

"Arrr well, she be only one of them thar pleasure schooners," said Captain Bold. "Yers, I can see now. There be crowds of jolly folk aboard sucking toffee-apples and fizzypops and a wearing Kiss-me-Quick cowboy hats. Brace yerselves, mates, while I ups the throttle to Full Speed Ahead and steams out of her way."

Then off we went racingly with lines of white water coming out the back of us. But we could not leave that schooner behind, not even with our throttle upped to the top.

Captain Bold called out, "Has she come round far enough for you to pick out her name yet, Mister Lookout?" So Stubbs said "ARK!" times 3, meaning *Ark-ark* Captain, the name of that schooner is... **The Seafarkx!**

"Well stap me in the scuppers and swab me sideways! Look-ee thar!" cried Captain Bold swearingly.

So we lookee-d thar and oh no! Off came the seaside clothes plus the Kiss-me-Quick hats. Away went the toffee-apples, down came the fancy flags, up went the covers, out came the cannons and up went... The Snarl and Wishbones

Oo-er, pirates!!!

Yours hidinginabarrely,

2 deckpaws and 1 deckbeak

Dear Mum and Dad,

Today was a busy 1. We did flying, then we did more hiding, then we did getting clapped.

The flying part was in the barrel we were hiding in. The pirates thought our barrel must be just full of fishes like the others, so they picked us up by a winch (strong pickupper) and dropped us down their hold (ship's tum). I said whisperingly to Smells and Stubbs, "No noise, case they come searching, Ok?"

I wanted us to wait till night-time and then creep out in the deep dark, but all of a suddenly we heard taptap taptap. It was some pirates having a gloat over their new booties. 1 of them said (weaselly voice), "Yum yum, Crusher, grilled sardines for supper tonight!"

Then the other 1 said wildboarly, **"We shall have a rare old party, Bluetooth. The cap'n says we can help him toast old Bold's toes after! Course, that's only for spite, seeing as he says he still knows nothing of Blackfur's treasure. Snort the man and snort again that we're no nearer finding it! But we shall toast Cap'n Bold's snorting toes just the same and then heave him over the side."**

Then they did a taptap on our lid and Smells said, "Be quiet, Mister Tappyhead!" So the pirates said, "Hoy! Oo zed dat?" So Smells said, "Not me, it was the naughty fishes said that!" So cubbish.

They took off our lid and grabbed hold of us harshly by our scruffs saying, "Ah-harr stowaways. Gotcha! Slam 'em in the snorting brig, ect."

Then we got clapped the pirate way (eg. in irons).

Yours chainedupply,

Little

PS Never mind, they have not found Blackfur's treasure yet, have they?

Dear Mum and Dad,

Do you know brigs? You get them downstairs in pirate ships. They are nice and dark and smelly. They are a bit like Lairs (no portholes), only you put captured creatures in them. They have a strong iron door with nice big locks on, plus bars. BUT (big but) they are a bit boring because you cannot get out of them.

You do not get fed tasty grub in the brig, only old bread and water,  bluck. Good thing there is many a lost rat down here. Loads of them do not know the Small Cave Trick. Handy, because along they come scuttlingly saying (skweeky voice), "Hello, we are looking for some bilge, can you show us where it is?"

So we say, "Yes, pop in this small cave but mind all the stalagmites and tites, bit sharp." Then they pop in your mouth, so you can just go choff, hmmm tasty.

Not much else happened today, only a SPLOOSH then a *cheer* and a **BANG BANG BANG**

I did not like those bangs. Loud noises by guns ect. are my worst thing. So Stubbs said to me "ARK!" times 2 meaning do not fret and frown, that was only to cheer Captain Bold getting *char*ked over the side I *ark*spect.

Then Smells got a bit whiny. He likes being chained up, but he likes watching people getting splooshed better. So he went SCReamy SCReam SCReam, like always, when he wants spoiling rotten. Then Crusher poked his snout through the bars. He is a tuff old boar, did I tell you that? He has got a fat head, sharp tusks, plus big shoulders like a moose. Also he has got SNORT tattooed on his forehead.

He thinks that makes him look 2 millium times fiercer, I bet. He said, " **shut your snorting traps you lubbers or you'll end up swabbing out Davy Jones's locker!**"
So rude.

I wonder who Davy Jones is. Also, I never knew lockers needed swabbing.

Yours interestedly,

Littly

Dear Mum and Dad,

Small Arrroooo! for us being out of the brig but not 3 loud wuns because I think Captain Froshus is going to kill us dead.

After our bread-and-watery breakfast, Crusher opened up the iron door saying, "Snort, look lively, you snorting captives, smarten up. You are off to see the Cap'n, snort." Then he threw a bucket of water over us saying, "Bathtime, 1st!" Sad to say, that crool bucket of water made Stubbs' parrot paint come off, plus it washed off my eyepatch and made Smells' moustache go wonky.

Then Bluetooth the Weasel made us do Stickupp Paws with his pistols. So up on to the top deck we clanked drippingly (wet chains), then along came a load of pirates saying, "Har har, you have had it now, ect."

But we did not go all wob and weakly, oh no! Up went my chin in the wolfly way and out went Smells' tongue going pppth ppppth. Stubbs said "ARK!" meaning I am not scared of Davy Jones, even if he has got the d*arkest lark*er ever. We went right up the back of the ship till we came to a posh oak door. Crusher shouted, "Prisoners, halt!" going taptap with his ~~nkuckle~~ nuckle (cannot spell it) on the notice saying:

CAPTAIN'S CABIN

Crusher opened the door and pushed us all in. We could not see much in that cabin, only spoons and glasses going flash on the table, plus a tall shadowy brute behind it. All because of him standing in front of a wide window, wide as the ship, also the sunshine bouncing off the waves blindingly.

Quick as a chick I remembered Uncle Bigbad's Wolf Rule of Badness Number 3: *Fib your head off.* So I said (piratey voice), "At your service, C-Cap'n Froshus, a-harr!"

Then I smelt a peppery smell and a soft voice came saying, "My boys, welcome aboard *The Seafox*, the quickest, slickest pirate ship afloat.

I am the notorious Captain Froshus. My mission
is to be the All-Time Terror of The Shivery Sea
and to find the lost treasure of Blackfur the
Backbiter. Something tells me that you know
things about him that are as yet unknown to me.
Remember, I show no mercy to any who cross
me or stand in my way. So, pay attention, my
boys. Look deep, deep into my eyes. Can you
really be of service to me or are you just spies?
Think carefully. The answer you give will
determine whether you sail with me, or swim
with the sharks!"

Yours thisisitly,

Dear Mum and Dad,

Good thing his eyes were in the deep shadow. It was so hard not to give in to him. But I tried my hardest, saying, "Good joke about spies, Cap'n! Me and my brother plus my parrot here, we be not spies, ah-harr. We be all harsh young sailors wanted by the Coastguard Pleece, grrr. We stowed away on *The Saucy Sardine* just so you might capture us and let us be in your crew doing Treasure Seeking ect.!"

Bluetooth said whiningly, "Bit small for outlaws, ain't you, matey? And how come your parrot looks more like some scrawny little crow after his bath!"

Stubbs said a brave "ARK! ARK!" meaning Pieces of *Ark*! Pieces of *Ark*! But Bluetooth's big chum, Crusher, said, "Snort!

What shall we do with them, skipper – heave 'em over the side and use 'em for target practice like wot we dun with Captain Bold?" Oo-er.

But Captain Froshus spoke softly, saying, "My boys, you look a little pale. Not surprising after your ordeal in the brig. Pray accept my apologies. I am surrounded by ruffians with appalling manners. Allow me to offer you a nourishing snack. I trust, being desperate young brutes and wanted sea-outlaws that you can be persuaded to accept treats from a stranger? Would anyone like to tell me all their secret information about Blackfur's Treasure and help themselves to a bull's eye...?"

Bull's eyes are Smells' favourite, so he said, "Me me me!" Then Captain Froshus said replyingly, "What an eager young chappy you are, in your smart sailor suit. And what an impressive moustache, if a little lopsided. Tell me, young sir, in return for a pawful of bull's eyes and the promise of a job as my personal cabin cub, what are you prepared to tell me?"

Answer, "Everything."

So now he is Cabin Cub and Cook's Helper, all because of getting bribed! Stubbs must leave my shoulder and be the Lookout in the Crow's Nest. It is right up the top of the tallest mast so miles 2 highupp for him I bet. And guess what job I have got? Captain Froshus said I could be the Head Cleaner. Good, I like bossing people about.

Still, it will not be long before Smells blabs all of our secret clues about Blackfur, and how he is our grate ancestor. Plus all about our portrait of him with his chest and his twisty stick. Also, that old Blackfur song you sent. Smells kept playing it all the time on his Walkwolf, so I bet he hasn't forgotten it.

> *Seek my treasure in the bay,*
> *Where the unicorn doth play!*
> *Those who seek without a map,*
> *Mind the teeth that snarl and snap!*
> *Lucky those who most do itch,*
> *Scratch, and lo, ye shall be rich!*

So a dew wunce morely. Soon it will be cheer, sploosh, bang bang bang over the side for us I bet.

Then Captain Froshus will get so rich, all the people will say, "Captain Froshus is our Top Terror of All Time. He makes grate wolves like Blackfur Wolf and Bigbad Wolf seem just tame weakies!"

Yours shamedly,

Little Wolf (not grate, sniff)

PS They were not even proper bull's eyes, they were just a trick, eg. mint sweeties with stripes on, yuck.

PPS I have just found out another trick. I am the Cleaner of the Head, not the Head Cleaner. Sad to say, the Head is the sailor word for the lav, so that is me pinged up times 2.

*Behind the Capstan (for pulling anchor up,
did you know?) The Seafox*

Dear Mum and Dad,

I am sooooo tired, phew. It has been scrub scrub scrub in the Head (lav) plus pirates calling me names all the time. Also the wind got up early (it was sleeping behind Vile Island). Then it found some rain to throw while giving the sea a shake, so all the pirates keep shouting out chantingly,

"Lubber,
the Scrubber,
we have done a sick!
Fetch-a,
your bucket,
and mop here quick!"

Big fuss today because of Stubbs not wanting to stay up The Crows Nest (2 giddy). He keeps hopping down the rigging to the crosstrees (sticks holding out the sails) saying "ARK!" meaning he wants to be the *lark*out from lower down. Now the Bosun is after him to give him a stinger with a short rope.

Captain Froshus has been trying and trying to get Treasure Clues off Smells by spoiling him rotten. I can see the steerywheel now, and guess who is getting a go at doing steering? Smells!

Also, not fair, he has got a big yellow oilskin hat and cloak on, so he can copy Captain Froshus and the Mate by looking posh and mysterious.

Now the Captain and the Mate are having a huddly look at the sea map, with hats pulled down darkly. The captain is saying to Smells, "Sing us your funny song, my boy! Then the  nice Mate and I can look on the chart and see if there are any places that match the words. Because if you are a helpful young chappy, you shall have a share of the treasure and be rich. Then you can buy a splendid little pirate ship of your own."

Smells says replyingly, "B Ọ Ọ m   b Ọ Ọ m   b Ọ Ọ m !" so Captain Froshus says, "Absolutely, my boy. You shall also have as many cannon as you wish. Now sing up!"

I will just pop this letter in a bottle for you (bit 2 wet), and start up another 1 quick.

yrs hastingly,

L

Dear Mum and Dad,

Good thing Smells is rubbish at singing.
Because when he sings the Blackfur song, it
comes out like this:

> Unicorns got the treasure,
> Don't wanna play.
> Snap snarl bay,
> Sickee sickee sickee,
> Itchy itchy Richy.

Now Captain Froshus is saying whisperingly to
the Mate, "Mostly cubbish nonsense of course. But
can you see a Snarl Bay on the chart? Or what
about Itchy Point? Or Unicorn
Something? What about
Unicorn Island?"

Smells is not taking
any notice because
of having a nice
sing. Plus a steer
of the ship, going
brrrm brrrm.

Aha! Now the Mate has seen something on the chart. He said, "There be a group of rocky islands here, Cap'n, a day or two's sailing to the East of Vile Isle. There be Parrot Island, Piggy Island and Narwhal Island. And here be a Narwhal Bay, look. No sign of Unicorn Island, though, Cap'n."

Now Captain Froshus is acting all feddup and snappish. Oh no! Here comes the Bosun with Stubbs under 1 arm saying, "Mutiny! This young crow be too frit to stay up in the Crow's Nest as ordered, Cap'n!"

Guess what the Captain just said snarlingly? He said "All paws and hoofs on deck to witness punishment! We shall have to teach this young coward a lesson. Fifty lashes should do the trick! Fetch the cat-o'-nine-tails!"

Yours mustdosomethingly,

Little

Dear Mum and Dad,

Sorry if this paper is even ~~smujjier rinklier~~ wetter than before. I have just found out what 'welking the plonk' is, Dad. And all because I did not want Stubbs getting lashes off a cat with nine tails.

All the pirates came up on deck saying, "Oh good, it has stopped raining nearly. We have not had a nice flogging all week, ect." Then along came the Bosun. He tied Stubbs to a ship's rail harshly, saying, "I be going to give you a taste of the cat-o'-nine-tails, my bird!" What a wopping big fibber about cats! He did not have a cat, just a whip instead, with all strings and ~~nkots nots~~ knots on it.

Then the sun bit a hole in the clouds, the drums went brrrr and up went the Bosun's strong right hand with the whip ready. So I jumped springingly on to the quarterdeck. I got out my cubscout knife, and cut Stubbs' ropes saying, "Fly for it, Stubby! You can do it!" Down

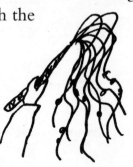

came the whip cracklingly but not quick enuff for a quick crowchick! Up went Stubbs flappingly. Bang bang bang bang went the anti-aircrow

guns, but Stubbs zigged off zaggingly saying "ARK!" times 3, meaning bad lark, I have arkscaped, you missed the mark!

Sad to say, I did not arkscape. All the pirates grabbed hold of me, saying, "Let us feed this 1 to the sharks Cap'n. Go on, else we shall not be having no crool fun at all today."

So the captain said softly, "Very well, you shall have your wicked way. Little Wolf – for I know it is he – is of no further use to me, and his baby brother is now entirely in my power. It is only a matter of time before Blackfur's treasure is mine! Over the side with the little brute and good riddance." Then he took off his yellow oilskin hat all of a suddenly and let me see his pointy face. Oh no, he was not Captain Froshus, he was Mister Twister the Fox!

Then the pirates made me stand on a short floorboard sticking over the side. I looked down saying, "Hoy, not fair, that is a long drop, plus look at all those sharks down there!" But they did not take any notice, they made me do a long walk, hurryingly, by pricking my bott with sharp points. Ooch, ouch, splooosh!

Yours nomorely,

Mister Ghostiecub

Dear Mum and Dad,

Smells did th

Good thing Smells got all jealous about me going sploosh. He wanted to have a sploosh 2. In he came splooshing on top of me in the salty water, holding his little wooden spoon that he got for being Cook's Helper.

Smells did t

Round and round us came a pack of hungry sharks. They showed us their big teeth just to make us go all frozz and stiff I bet. But I said, "Back to back, Smells, come on. We will show these sea-wolves how land-wolves can fight!" Then me and Smells made a wopping splash saying sternly, "Shove off you big bullies, or you will all get a harsh poke up the nosehole, no messing grrr!"

Smells did

Getting poked up the nosehole is a shark's worst thing, did you know that? So well done us for tricky braveness! Then we saw all the pirates leaning over the side shouting, "Snort and blust it! The blinking blunkers be still alive. Get the muskets! Run out the bow chaser! Target practice!" Then it was **BANG** **BANG** **BANG** **BOOM** for a bit but they could not hit a flea, lucky for us. Plus, all of a soonly, the wind blew the other way and made them sail away from us. Arrroooo!

Away and away blew *The Seafox*. Then guess what? It fell off the edge of the sea. Arrrooo! Serves them right. So then there was just me and Smells left floating on top of all the wide part of the sea. I said, "DYB DOB Smells, let us do a fast eastly swim. If we do not get eaten or drowned, maybe we will come to an island, yes?"

smells did this

Smells got all whiny saying, "I hate sea, I only like pirate ships." So I said, "Never mind, Smells, DYB DOB and keep cubbypaddling till we come to some nice brown land, then we can scrape out a small lair to have a rest in. Plus you can do writing on my letter if you like. I am sending this to Mum and Dad in my last bottle, OK?"

Smells did th

So the posh writing is mine plus Smells did the cubbish skribbully bits.

Yours floatingly,

Little and Smells

PS We had to take the letter out of the bottle again to do a short PS.
PPS The PS is that Stubbs has come back, Arrroooo! He went to look for land. He found some (not 2 far as the crow flaps), but he is feeling arksaucested. So now he is sitting on my head guidingly.

Land!

Dear Mum and Dad,

Oo-er! We keep getting killed nearly, but not by sharks. By other sharp teeth!

Cubbypaddling is hard if you are only a small weaky like Smells. Also, even if you have got tuff mussels like me, hem hem. Good thing I had Stubbs on my head because every time my eyelids went click, he went "ARK!" meaning keep aw*ark*! Keep t*ark*ing.

But then we did not have the strongness in our legs for more kicking. I felt very down and dumply. But Stubbs flapped his wings, saying "ARK!" meaning h*ark*, pay *ark*tention. So we h*ark*ed. 1st we heard a ᴚᴀᴀʜʜ, like that, only soon it got more like a **ᴿᴀᴀAH**.

You think it was lions or tigers, I bet? But no, it was big waves hurting themselves on many a sharp black rock. I said, "Wake up, Smells. Rocks! Plus there is an island on the other side of them. Arrroooo!"

Smells did not open his eyes. I said, "Do your cubbypaddle, Smells, else you might go under or get bashed on the rocks!" Just then I saw 2 big shadows coming up from deep down in the water. I thought oh no, those sharks are crafty, they are waiting till we fall asleep then they will crunch us up!

Stubbs said, "ARK!" meaning lookout, sh*arks*!" But then came a whistly voice saying, "Hello, you furry boys. Hop on our backs if you want a lift."

Yours holdtightly,

Little Cowboy

Dear Mum and Dad,

That was porpoises picked us up on their
backs, not sharks. They are such good swimmers,
faster than ships, I bet. They are like sea
cubscouts. They like doing a good turn every day
(eg. opposite of Uncle Bigbad's Rule of Badness
Number 6, *Do your dirtiest every day*). Handy, eh?

The porpoises carried us straight for the rocks,
doing their whistling. We thought oh no, soon we
will be like cubby kebabs on those sharp points!
But no, those porpoises can dodge and jump about
1 millium miles high! Over some rocks we went
leapingly. Also we went through some gaps
skweezingly – till we came into a bay. The nice
porpoises laid us down on the warm
sand. We whistled byebye and $z_{z_{z_{z_{z_z}}}}$ fast asleep.

Morningtime now. We are alive still.
But Macarooned!

Yours wideyely,

The Wolf Bruvs
(plus Stubbs)

Dear Mum and Dad,

Here is my riddle for today (instead of Boring News).

What goes:

" wsHHHHHh wsHHHHHh *plop plop*
pinck pinck skwaark.? "

Answer: an island. Did you get it? The first part is waves. No, the next bit is not rude. It is big hollow nuts going plop on your head if you sit under their trees for a cooloff.
Next bit is crabs (tasty), and
the last bit is parrots ect.

I am sitting on the sand having a hard think about what islands Captain Froshus' mate said he found on his chart. Wun was Parrot Island. Then he said Piggy Island. Then there was a funny name but, sad to say, I cannot remember.

So maybe this 1 we are on is Parrot Island. Or is it Piggy Island? We have not smelt any piggies yet, boo shame, but maybe they live up the hill in the jungly part. Tomorrow I am going for a long *arks*plore with Stubbs.

Smells says he wants to stay on the beach and do digging (his best favourite thing 1 time, remember?). He is xcited because of finding a load of old brown bottles in the sand saying RUM in old writing. They smell all funny, a bit like Uncle Bigbad's whisky bottle when he was a ghostie spirit.

But it is v. good because bottles are handy for posting letters. Plus for bonking snacks on the head, eg. crabs, limpets, winkles, nuts ect.

Yours desertislandly,

The Castaway

Dear Mum and Dad,

Stubbs and me had a good old *ark*splore today.
Right up the top of the hill I went in-and-out-
of-the-palmtreesly. Stubbs was teaching all the
parrots to say "ARK!" It is easy cheesy for them
because they are quick copiers. If you say to
them, "Hello flashywings, say
inkywinkypinkybeak," they say it back.

When we got up the top we could see all
round. So there you are, this is deffnly an island.
It is all green (my best colour), with yellow and
black round the edges.

We spied another bay next
to our 1. It looked like a small
bite out of the island. There
was many a black rock guarding
it, more than in our bay even.

We could just see a big something swimming in the water on the other side of those rocks. We thought, hmmm, a big fish, miles more big than porpoises even. He was sliding along like a shadow, then diving down, then coming up for a gasp. So we thought, aha, a whale. But guess what? He had a huge long spiky spike sticking out of his face! I said, "Oo-er, it's a seamonster!"

We called out to Smells to run round the edge of the island and look. He likes monsters. But he was 2 busy digging or 2 far away to hear.

There is not 1 smell of a piggy but plenty of wiggly snacks, kwite tasty. So I do not think this can be Piggy Island. Must be Parrot Island. Or that other island I have forgotten the name of.

Yours sherlockly,

The Workitouter

Dear Mum and Dad,

I am writing this by misty moonlight – deep breath, steady steady.

You will not beLEEEEV what Smells has dug up now! Loads of cannons, plus pistols, muskets, flints, tinderboxes, gunpowder, cannonballs, small bullets, swords ect. PLUS (big plus) a load of pirate costumes, also blankets in a trunk! Arrroooo! Are these from our ancestor Blackfur the Backbiter, I wonder? Because then maybe his treasure is somewhere on this island 2! Maybe this *is* the island with the funny name that we can't remember?

Smells went mad doing his digging in the sand all day, so holes *everywhere* round here. But still not 1 bit of gold or jewels yet, boo shame. Tomorrow we will all go and have a dig next door in Monster Bay (I made that name up, do you like it?) BUT (big but), even if we find the treasure, how can we get it home?

Yours still macaroonedly,

Littly

PS Good thing the gunpowder is damp. Smells has found out how you get sparks off a tinderbox so he wants to be Mister Clicky and blow it all up in 1 go.

Monster Bay, just round the corner from Our Bay,
Somewhere Island, Notsurewhat Sea

Dear Mum and Dad,

We woke up today – still all
misty. So we had a snack
of sea urchins. They're a
bit like hedgehogs only
scruffier, so it is bonk
with a rum bottle then
mind your paws and nose.

Then off we went paddlingly round the corner
to the next bay.

Smells came 2. He was
hoping we might see the
seamonster wunce
morely. We took pistols
tucked up our shorts.
But the gunpowder was
still damp so we had to
do pretend shooting
saying, "Pchhh Pchhhh
got you, roll over you are
dead."

It was kwite hard seeing (mist) so when we got to that next bay, we could not see even out to the shocking rocks. So Stubbs said "ARK!" meaning let us try an *ark*speriment of doing a wissul in the water through a hollow bamboo. Then maybe those kind porpoises would come and xplain. Eg. "Has the seamonster got any bad hobbies?" Answer, "Yes, he likes eating macarooners, ect."

Just then the mist started melting. Smells pointed out to the sea saying, "Look, pirates coming, ppchhh pchhh you are dead!" So we had a long look and yes, there was a sailing boat coming. It was only a small sailing 1, so you will think, "Good, it was not *The Seafox* then." Ah, but it *was* flying The Snarl and Wishbones!

I said, "Down flat everybody, and no going pchhhh, Smells! We must hide out of the way, in case of getting killed by cannonballs!"

The boat pointed itself at the rocks, trying to find a way through them. Down came the sail and then—

"ARK!" said Stubbs, meaning Seamonster Att*ark*!

All of a zoomingly the seamonster came up out the water like a big rock come to life! He went crashingly over the waves, pointing his sharp spike at the side of the boat! We shouted out "Arrroooo!!" and "ARK!" Plus dancing about 4 being saved from the pirates, but then **BASH!** The seamonster went flying out of the water! Round he went spinningly, half of his spike knocked off. Then down he dived, all shamed.

That was when the boat went **CRUNCH** on to the rocks.

Yours shockedly,

Littly

Dear Mum and Dad,

Bit boring today. Not really, only joking! Because it was not pirates in that boat, it was Normus Bear and Yeller come to help us!!

Normus was the 1 who grabbed hold of the seamonster's spike that was going to sink the boat. Also, when he gave the seamonster a hard bash, ½ the spike busted off in his paw. So the seamonster went back down the deep going, "Boohoo, blub blum, I want my mum." Normus gave the spike to Yeller for a present. Sad to say, then the boat got stuck on the rocks. So into the seawater jumped Normus with Yeller on his back. Strong as King Kong he came swimmingly to the shore right up to us!

Out of the water they rushed with a shake and a splash. We were all so happy we had a fun restle, even Stubbs. I said, "Arrroooo! I thought you 2 were in a grump with me 4 leaving you behind."

But Yeller yelled, replyingly, "DO NOT BE DAFT, LICKLE! WE ARE YOUR CHUMS, WE WOULD NEVER LET YOU DOWN."

Then we had a chase, plus a roll in the sand till our pants got so fast we could not speak. But then Stubbs said "ARK!" meaning that the seamonster's spike was *ark*zactly like Blackfur the Backbiter's walking stick.

Yeller said a shouting, "YES, THAT WAS A CLUE IN BLACKFUR'S PORTRAIT." Also he said that when he found out where that twisty stick came from, he found out what the 1st clue in the Blackfur song meant!

I will xplain that clue to you soonly by rum bottle. Also I will say how he worked out what the Blackfur song means. But no more writing today, I just want to have FUN!

Your cheery boy,

Littly

Dear Mum and Dad,

Arrroooo! We are hot on the trail of Blackfur the Backbiter's treasure. Now I will say how.

You know when me and Stubbs had to do Running Away To Sea swiftly and Yeller and Normus were sposed to stay and look after Smells? Well, as soon as they found out Smells was not in bed with the chickypops, Yeller had a good think. He thought, "HMMMM, WE MUST GO AND FIND SMELLS AND HELP LICKLE. WHICH WAY DID THEY GO?" Then he thought, "I KNOW! LICKLE HAS GOT A SHARP DETECTY BRANE SO SOON HE WILL BE ON THE TRAIL OF BLACKFUR THE

BACKBITER'S TREASURE. I BETTER THINK UP A GOOD IDEA OF FINDIN A SHORTCUT, CASE LICKLE, SMELLS AND STUBBS GET IN TROUBLE, MAYBE WITH CAPTAIN FROSHUS EVEN."

Then he had a long look at Blackfur's portrait and all of a suddenly— "DING! I KNOW WHERE I HAVE SEEN A TWISTY STICK LIKE BLACKFUR IS HOLDIN. IT WAS IN MY BOOK I WAS READIN CALLED *Shocking Brute Beasts of the Deep and Dark.* SO I HAD A FLIP THROUGH THE PAGES AND YES, THERE WERE FINE PICS OF WHALES. THERE WERE SPERM WUNS, KILLER WUNS, BLUE WUNS ect. BUT (BIG BUT) THERE WAS A FUNNY WUN WITH A BIG LONG SPIKE STUCK ON HIS FACE. THE WRITIN SAID UNDERNEATH:

THE NARWHAL OR SEA UNICORN

"SO THEN I THOUGHT, DING! IT SAYS ABOUT UNICORNS AND TREASURE IN BLACKFUR'S SONG!"

I said, "Aha, Yeller, I know the part you mean:

Seek my treasure in the bay,
Where the unicorn doth play!"

Then we had to let
Smells sing that song
in his funny way
about 1 millium
times, till he got a
coff—

Coff

Yours backinamoly,

I. M. Bustin (get it?)

Dear M and D,

Phew, phew, that's better. Sorry.

When it was all quiet, eg. when Smells had stopped coffing, Normus said, "Yes, Yeller remembered the words in that part of the song too. So we got out a big map of all Beastshire and Grimshire, plus the Seas, to look for Narwhals or Unicorns. And faraway to the east in The Sea of Sultriness, we found Narwhal Island and Narwhal Bay."

Yeller said, "YEAH. SO THEN WE NIPPED OFF QUICK AS A CHICK TO THE SHIVERY SEA, BORROWED A BOAT AND SAILED HERE AS FAST AS WE COULD."

"It was my idea to fly the Snarl and Crossbones," said Normus proudly. "I know we are not pirates really, but I wanted the flag to say, '*We only look small but watch it, we are hard bashers!*'"

"BIG SHAME WE DID NOT HAVE A PROPER CHART OF NARWHAL ISLAND TO SHOW US A WAY THROUGH THE ROCKS, THOUGH!" Yeller yelled sadly.

"Aha! Those *rocks* are the teeth that snarl and snap, I bet!" I said. Then I sang the clue from Blackfur's song:

"Those who seek without a map,
Mind the teeth that snarl and snap!"

So, Mum and Dad, that means the *last* part of the song has also got an important clue in it. But now we are all having a nice lie-down on the beach under the stars. Maybe after a good rest we will all wake up more clever.

Yours curledupcontently,

L Wolf and Co Ltd

Narwhal Bay, Narwhal Island, The Sea of Sultriness

Dear Mum and Dad,

Cor, what a scratchy night we had. It was sandfleas. They made us go itch itch all the time, boo shame.

Those sandfleas got Normus's temper up. That is Y he got up very early and started bashing the sand saying, "I hate Narwhal Bay! It is itchier than an itchy ants' nest!" That made Smells start copying him, by throwing sand all over.

Then all of a suddenly Yeller and me went DING! together. Plus we started singing the last part of the song together eg.

"Lucky those who most do itch,
Scratch, and lo, ye shall be rich!"

"I GET IT, LICKLE!" yelled Yeller. "THE
CLUE MEANS YE MUST SCRATCH YE
SAND, NOT SCRATCH YE *FUR*, IF YE
WANT TO GET RICH!"

So we all went dig dig in the sand of Narwhal
Bay. It was hot work with the sun on our heads
but we did not stop. Then I felt a hard thing
under my claws. I thought, "This is a big rock."
But it was not a rock, it was a big chest.

Arrroooo! I howled to the others and they all
came and helped. We scratched and scratched in
the sand until we could pull that big chest out!
Normus gave the lock a hard bash. Up went the lid.

And look, I have done you a nice pic of us having a pretend wash with all the gold and jewels inside!

Yours gloatingly

Little and Chums

PS Only prob is, how do we get it back to the Lair 4 you? (No boat)

Narwhal Bay, Narwhal Island, The Sea of Sultriness

Dear Mum and Dad,

It is nice being rich, but not if you are macarooned for ever and ever. It is rubbish having a load of jewels ect. if you cannot ever go home and have your own bedroom wallpaper, plus tons of scary fun in a proper deep dark forest.

So this is our plan. We are going to send a message to *The Seafox* saying:

"Help Seafox, we ~~spender, surenda~~, give up. We have found the treasure and you can have it. BUT (big but) only if you take us back home to the far shore of Beastshire. PS Be nice, we are not many."

Good 1, yes?

Yours giveupply,

L ect.

Dear Mum and Dad,

1 big prob about giving up. How do we get the message to Captain Froshus? (Mister Twister really.)

Answer: Stubbs!

His tail feathers that Smells pinched off him have grown back (a bit). So we said how about him flying to *The Seafox*, holding our message in his beak? That made him go all trembly. He said "ARK?" meaning what about hur*rark*anes and sh*ark*s ect.?

I said, "Stubbs, you have been a fine trick parrot. Plus you *ark*scaped from the pirates' anti-aircrow fire, plus you guided me and Smells to Narwhal Island. I am your Pirate Cheef saying, "Stubby Crow, you are a hero already, plus you are only small. So only go if you want to, OK?"

Out went Stubbs' small chest. He said a soft "ARK!" meaning *ark*ay Cheef, and do not be wurrid, I will be b*ark*! And off he flapped nobly over the rocks, till he was just like a small full stop, eg.

It is a bit windy, so paws crossed he does not crash in The Sea of Sultriness (sharks).

Yours hopingforthebestly,

Little

Dear Mum and Dad,

Stubbs has been gone 4 many a bright moon. Maybe he is a bit 2 weaky to reach *The Seafox*, BUT (big but), me and my small pirate crew must get ready DYB DOB DYBly. I have done you a list of stuff we must do, just in the small case of Stubbs' wings having the strongness to flap him all the way to that ship with our message.

List of Must Do Stuff

 Cannons. Drag (well, Normus mostly) the cannons ect. round to Narwhal Bay.

 Hide them under some old blankets (sand colour).

Take tinder box off smells for a short time, then finish drying out all the gunpowder.

127

Dress up in the old pirate clothes we found, plus put on loads of swords, daggers, cutlasses (not cute lasses, Dad) pistols, ect. in belts made spesh to hold them. I get to wear the Pirate Cheef's (eg. Blackfur's) costume: hat with a mutton bones badge made out of all sparkly jewels, earring ect.

 Tuck fuses under my pirate hat for a big shock later.

Me and Yeller and Normus put on boots with xtra thick soles.

 Jump skweezingly into our 3 biggest cannons for the practiss.

ho ho Sing Ho yoyo ect. a lot in harsh whisper for the practiss, plus crewspirit.

Arrroooo! Did you think, "Oh no. The shame. Our boy is going to surrender to Mister Twister?" I bet you did. But NO! That was a **Trick Message** we sent to trick him, only shhhh, case of him finding out.

Yours waitandseely,

Blackfur the Backbiter the 2nd, Pirate Cheef

Dear Mum and Dad,

I am not saying "Nar Nar", in case you might nip me sharply. But today we are glad I did not listen to you saying, "Grrrr, pack up doing reading and Pirate Practiss!" Because they helped a *lot*!

At sunjumpup we saw *The Seafox* come sailing sneakingly up to the rocks but not crashing boo shame (big anchor). All the pirates were on deck looking for us. They could see the treasure chest on the beach, but not us hiding craftily under Blackfur's blankets.

Mister Twister spoke to us through his loudshouter, saying (soapy voice), "Ahoy there, my boys. Captain Froshus speaking – where are you? Do not fret and fear. Come out and show yourselves! I have received and understood your message, well done. How wise to surrender to me. I am, after all, the biggest Terror of All Time! Your messenger, the crow, is exhausted but safe. I have him tied to a hammock in my sick bay. He shall come to no harm and of *course* we shall be nice to *you*, provided there are no tricks. Wait where you are while we lower a boat. We shall collect the treasure and then come back and collect you."

I whispered, "You will not trick us with your foxy ways, Mister Twister! Ready Yeller? Ready, Normus? It is time to give him some SST! Stand by to remove blankets, Smells. Go!"

131

Off came the blankets and into the cannons we popped.

We could hear the pirates give a big loud laugh, thinking we were trying to hide like rabbits. They did not know about Surprise Speed and Terror waiting 4 them!

Yours whizzingly,

The Faymuss Furry Cannonballs

Dear Mum and Dad,

Good firing Smells! He never misses!

Into the rigging flew us
Furry Cannonballs. All the
fuses under my hat were
smoking, so down I came
like a big scary cloud full
of thunder, shooting
pistols going "Graaaah!"

Out came my trusty cubscout penknife. Out
came Yeller's cutlass and out came Normus's 2-
pawed sword. Down the ratlines we went
swingingly with a slosh and a slash.
Snip went the ropes holding up
the sails. Normus was on the
deck most swiftly, so he did
Swashing, Buckling and Bashing
all round. BANG went
Bluetooth. BIFF went the Bosun.
CRASH went Crusher. Then
Sploosh, Sploosh, Splooosh! All of them
went over the side!

The rest of the pirates went "HELP, WHAT BE HAPPENING?" Because down came the sails on top of them. So:

1. They could not see proply.
2. They got tangled like sardines in a net.
3. When the cannons went off bang they got a coff from the smoke.
4. They got a hard bash by Normus if they did not surrender quick!

Across the deck I came swingingly on a rope saying (gruff voice), "Where be Captain Froshus, or should I say, Mister Twister the Fox? Ah-harrr! You have upsett the wolfly spirit of the Greatest Terror of the Sea Ever. So here I be, the shocking spirit of Blackfur the Backbiter come to haunt you and your crew of cowardy custards!"

Your victorious Pirate Cheef,

Little Seawolf

Dear Mum and Dad,

Do you know paw-to-paw combat? I have just had some with Mister Twister.

Normus and Yeller put all the pirate prisoners in lifeboats. Yeller shouted a good joke at them, "ROW AWAY AND DO NOT COME BACK!" Just then our Gunner (or Smells really) started firing cannonballs that did wopping big splooshes near them in the water, so away they went swiftly like daddylonglegs.

Then up from the sickbay jumped Mister Twister, all covered up in armour. He had a big iron helmet on, also an iron jacket plus iron pants to keep him safe.

He had a pistol in 1 paw and Stubbs tucked under the other, saying, "You may have fooled those miserable weasels and wild boars with your pistols and your fizzing fuses but you cannot fool a fox. I know you are *not* Blackfur The Backbiter, Former Terror of All the Seas. You are just that scrawny Little Wolf. Now hand over the treasure to me or say farewell to your crowchick friend."

I said gulpingly, "How about if we have a fight, paw-to-paw, for Stubbs and the treasure instead?"

So Mister Twister put Stubbs down saying, "Certainly, my boy." Only he did not say he was going to have a big long sword, and me only with my trusty cubscout penknife.

I said, "That is a crafty 1, but be careful, my penknife has got a spiky thing for digging stones out of horse's hoofs. Wait 1 mo, it is a bit stiff."

But he would not wait fairly, he came rushing at me cheatingly with a swoosh, saying "Take that, Master Backbiter!"

Just then Smells went **BANG** with his blunderbuss from the beach. It was a long way away, but do you know something? A musket ball went snip through Mister Twister's braces. Down on the deck went his iron pants, DONK! Quick as a chick I went rushingly up behind him and gave him a sharp nip on the you-know-what. Har har!

Mister Twister went "EEEEEK!" like a big baby mousy. Then he went over the side. Splooosh!

Normus said, "Catch this lifebelt, Mister Twister. And keep splashing, because look, a big shark is after you!"

Yeller said, "GOOD WORK, LICKLE, OR SHOULD. I CALL YOU LICKLE BLACKFUR?"

Yours winningly,

LB the BB

Posh Table, Captain's Cabin, The Seawolf (hem hem),
The Shivery Sea, Near The Coast of Beastshire

Dear Mum and Dad,

This is the last letter I am sending by bottle.
My next 1 will be by envelope. Arrroooo!

Sad to say, you are not rich yet, eg. no treasure
4 you. Y? Answer, here is a clue:

Guess who that small
sailor is, cuddling the
treasure chest? He is
saying, "Hello all my
darling gold and
jewels, you are
mine kiss kiss."
We had to let him
be the owner of them because he kept going
round letting off all the cannons so our ears went
ding. Plus it was because of you always saying,
"Give in to him, it is the only way." So we did.

Never mind. I 'spect you are ever so cheery
about me getting back the proud name of Wolf
by capturing a ship off a crafty fox, yes?

Here's a pic of us having a fine life on the ocean wave, on the good ship *Seawolf* (our posh new name, hem hem). That is me being the Captain. Normus is the 1 doing the fishing. Yeller is the 1 shouting, "COR I CAN SEE A MONSTER IN THIS TELESCOPE," (Only it is Stubbs looking at him down the other end really!)

Maybe Smells will bring his riches with him to the Lair if you let him come back and be your cabin cub. Only joking, not really. He wants to stay with me and Yeller and Normus and Stubbs *for ages*. Not just because he knows we are the best crew ever.

It is because SST is Smells' best thing now. Plus he knows our Big Plan. I will say it to you in the next letter, if you like.

Yours temptingly,

Captain L. Wolf,
Terror of the The Shivery Sea

Dear Mum and Dad,

Here is that something you are dying to know about, I bet.

The **Big** Plan

When me, Normus, Yeller, Stubbs and Smells get to the land, we are going to make a wopping trolley and put the *Seawolf* on it. Then we are going to push it all the way back to Frettnin Forest and do a lawnch of it on Lake Lemming! Then we will call the big old house that used to belong to Uncle Bigbad, Adventure Academy again. We will put up this notice saying:

Calling all slow weakies
Come and learn SST (surprise Speed and Terror) off me and my faymuss Pirate crew!
Have a free sail in the good ship SEAWOLF that we captured off Captain Froshus (Mister Twister).
Bags of Bangs, Clangs Tricks and Fun.
Signed Little Blackfur

Arrroooo! for the pirate crew!

Shock on the Shivery Sea: Wolves Are Top Terrors Again

For far too long, Wolves have faced relegation from the Premier League of Crookedness and Cunning. But NOT ANY MORE! says top reporter, Lurker P Wolf.

Recent opinion polls among the brute beasts of Frettnin Forest awarded wolves a shaming 3 out of 10 for Slipperiness and Slybootery, and a mere 2 for Terror! Asked the question, "Who put the shiver in the The Shivery Sea?" 99% of our readers ticked the *Captain Froshus* box.

Well now, thanks to Little Wolf, his bothersome brother, Smellybreff, and their courageous chums Yeller Wolf, Normus Bear and Stubby Crow, all that has changed. Lupines are back on top of the Terror Tables and the mighty pirate Captain Froshus has been exposed as none other than the foxy Master of Disguises – Mister Twister.

Read how Twister and his huge harsh crew were captured and put to flight by just five ferocious fluffballs.

Read how Little Wolf's exploits outshone those of his great ancestor Blackfur the Backbiter.

Read how he earned the even more fearsome name of:

BLACKFUR THE BOTTOM BITER!

Order Form

To order direct from the publishers, just make a list of the titles you want and fill in the form below:

Name ....

Address ....

....

....

Send to: Dept 6, HarperCollins Publishers Ltd,
Westerhill Road, Bishopbriggs, Glasgow G64 2QT.

Please enclose a cheque or postal order to the value of the cover price, plus:

UK & BFPO: Add £1.00 for the first book, and 25p per copy for each additional book ordered.

Overseas and Eire: Add £2.95 service charge. Books will be sent by surface mail but quotes for airmail despatch will be given on request.

A 24-hour telephone ordering service is available to holders of Visa, MasterCard, Amex or Switch cards on 0141- 772 2281.